Hairy Maclary Favourites

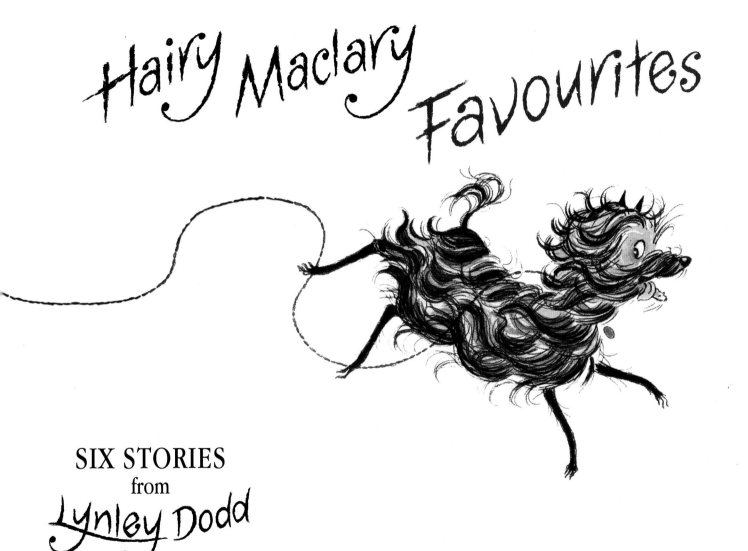

SIX STORIES
from
Lynley Dodd

PUFFIN BOOKS
Published by the Penguin Group
Penguin Group (NZ), 67 Apollo Drive, Rosedale,
Auckland 0632, New Zealand (a division of Pearson New Zealand Ltd)

Penguin Books Ltd, Registered Offices: 80 Strand, London, WC2R 0RL, England

This edition first published by Puffin Books, 2012
10 9 8 7 6

Hairy Maclary from Donaldson's Dairy
First published by Mallinson Rendel Publishers Ltd, 1983
Copyright © Lynley Dodd, 1983
Hairy Maclary's Bone
First published by Mallinson Rendel Publishers Ltd, 1984
Copyright © Lynley Dodd, 1984
Hairy Maclary Scattercat
First published by Mallinson Rendel Publishers Ltd, 1985
Copyright © Lynley Dodd, 1985
Hairy Maclary's Hat Tricks
First published by Mallinson Rendel Publishers Ltd, 2007
Copyright © Lynley Dodd, 2007
Hairy Maclary's Rumpus at the Vet
First published by Mallinson Rendel Publishers Ltd, 1989
Copyright © Lynley Dodd, 1989
Hairy Maclary, SHOO
First published by Mallinson Rendel Publishers Ltd, 2009
Copyright © Lynley Dodd, 2009

Copyright © Lynley Dodd, 1983, 1984, 1985, 2007, 1989, 2009

Printed in China through Colorcraft Ltd., Hong Kong

ISBN 978-0-143-50558-7

A catalogue record for this book is available from the National
Library of New Zealand.

www.penguin.co.nz

CONTENTS

Hairy Maclary

from Donaldson's Dairy

Out of the gate
and off for a walk
went Hairy Maclary
from Donaldson's Dairy

and Hercules Morse
as big as a horse

with Hairy Maclary
from Donaldson's Dairy.

Bottomley Potts
covered in spots,
Hercules Morse
as big as a horse

and Hairy Maclary
from Donaldson's Dairy.

Muffin McLay
like a bundle of hay,
Bottomley Potts
covered in spots,
Hercules Morse
as big as a horse

and Hairy Maclary
from Donaldson's Dairy.

Bitzer Maloney
all skinny and bony,
Muffin McLay
like a bundle of hay,
Bottomley Potts
covered in spots,
Hercules Morse
as big as a horse

and Hairy Maclary
from Donaldson's Dairy.

Schnitzel von Krumm
with a very low tum,
Bitzer Maloney
all skinny and bony,
Muffin McLay
like a bundle of hay,
Bottomley Potts
covered in spots,
Hercules Morse
as big as a horse

and Hairy Maclary
from Donaldson's Dairy.

With tails in the air
they trotted on down
past the shops and the park
to the far end of town.
They sniffed at the smells
and they snooped at each door,
when suddenly,
out of the shadows
they
saw …

SCARFACE CLAW
the toughest Tom
in
town.

"EEEEEOWWWFFTZ!"
said Scarface Claw.

Off with a yowl
a wail and a howl,
a scatter of paws
and a clatter of claws,
went Schnitzel von Krumm
with a very low tum,
Bitzer Maloney
all skinny and bony,
Muffin McLay
like a bundle of hay,
Bottomley Potts
covered in spots,
Hercules Morse
as big as a horse

and Hairy Maclary
from Donaldson's Dairy,

straight back home
to bed.

Hairy Maclary's Bone

Down in the town
by the butcher's shop door,
sat Hairy Maclary
from Donaldson's Dairy.

Out of the door
came Samuel Stone.
He gave Hairy Maclary
his tastiest
bone.

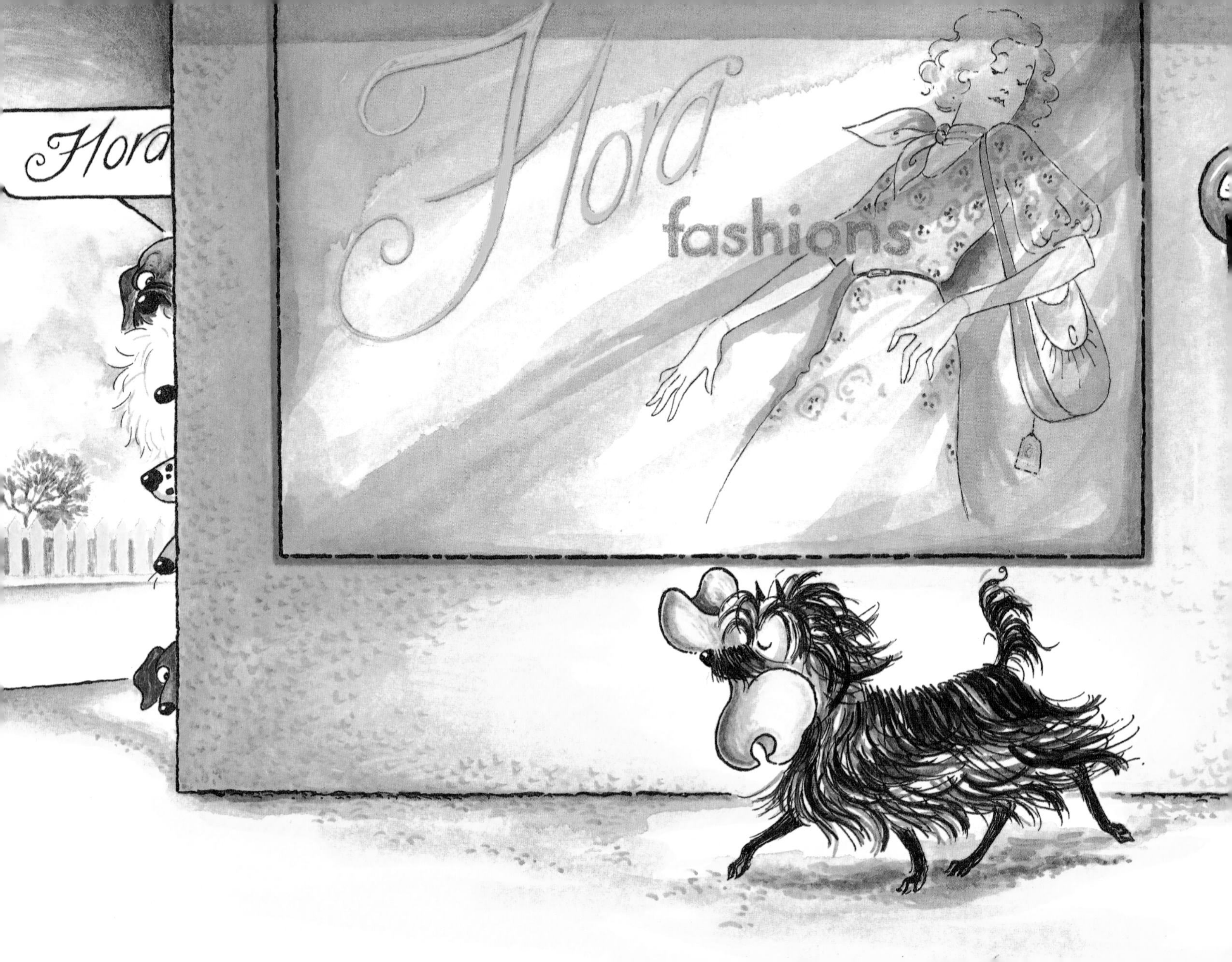
Flora
Flora
fashions

Then off up the street
on scurrying feet,
on his way to the dairy
went Hairy Maclary.

And chasing him home,
with their eyes on the bone,
went Hercules Morse,
Bottomley Potts,
Muffin McLay,
Bitzer Maloney
and Schnitzel von Krumm
with the very low tum.

Hungrily sniffing
and licking their chops,
they followed him up
past the school and the shops.

They came to the sign
selling Sutherland's Sauce.
Through they all went —

except Hercules Morse.

They came to a hedge
along Waterloo Way.
Under they went —

except Muffin McLay.

They came to a yard
full of dinghies and yachts.
Round they all went —

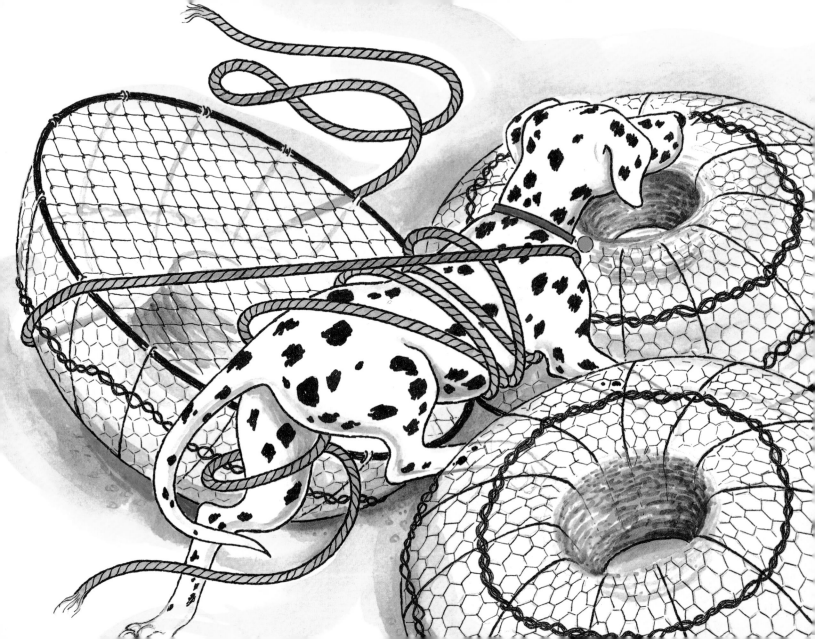

except Bottomley Potts.

They came to a building site,
cluttered and stony.
Over they went —

except Bitzer Maloney.

They came to a wall
by the house of Miss Plum.
One of them jumped —

but not Schnitzel von Krumm.

So at last he was free
to go home on his own,
Hairy Maclary
with ALL of his
bone.

Hairy Maclary Scattercat

Hairy Maclary
felt bumptious and bustly,
bossy and bouncy
and frisky and hustly.
He wanted to run.
He wanted to race.
But the MAIN thing he wanted
was something
to
chase.

Greywacke Jones
was hunting a bee.

BUT ALONG CAME HAIRY MACLARY …

and chased her up high
in the sycamore tree.

Butterball Brown
was washing a paw.

BUT ALONG CAME HAIRY MACLARY …

and bustled him under
a rickety door.

Pimpernel Pugh
was patting a ball.

BUT ALONG CAME HAIRY MACLARY ...

and chased her away
over Pemberton's wall.

Slinky Malinki
was down in the reeds.

BUT ALONG CAME HAIRY MACLARY …

and hustled him into
a drum full of weeds.

Mushroom Magee
was asleep on a ledge.

BUT ALONG CAME HAIRY MACLARY …

and chased her away
through a hole in the hedge.

Down on the path
by an old wooden rail,
twitching a bit,
was the tip of a tail.
With a bellicose bark
and a boisterous bounce,
Hairy Maclary
was ready
to
POUNCE

BUT AROUND CAME SCARFACE CLAW …

who bothered
and bustled him,
rustled and hustled him,
raced him
and chased him

ALL the way
home.

Hairy Maclary's Hat Tricks

SWOOOSH
went the wind
in the tops of the trees,
swishing the branches
and tossing the leaves.
It whipped around corners
and blew over bins,
it buffeted birds
into spirals and spins.
A blusterous, gusterous,
dusterous day,
but Hairy Maclary
was ready
to play.

He scooped up his skimmer
and carried it down
to the edge of the park
at the far end of town.
The wind was so restless,
its buffets so strong,
that it flapped him
and slapped him
and zapped him
along.

He waited for someone
to stop
and to play ...

but everyone said,
'We're TOO BUSY
today!'

Along came Miss Plum.
She patted his nose.
'Maybe,' she said,
'just a couple of throws.'

WHIZZ
went the skimmer
and off like a shot,
went Hairy Maclary,
post-haste,
from the spot.
He hurtled so fast
over pathway and creek,
that his legs were a blur
and his tail was
a streak.

THEN
with a swoop
and a flurry of black,
he caught it
and carried it
ALL the way
back.

ZING
went the skimmer,
high over a seat,
but Hairy Maclary
had wings on his feet.
He zoomed like a rocket,
he galloped and sped,
over railings and grass
and begonia bed.

THEN
with a swoop
and a flurry of black,
he caught it
and carried it
ALL the way
back.

Up at the top
in the summery sun,
the wind was enjoying
some frolicsome fun.
It played with the hats,
all the dresses
and veils,
it hassled the hairdos
and tangled
the tails.

Grandmother Pugh
was a vision in blue,
from the top of her head
to the bow on her shoe.
Her hat was a riot
of ribbon and lace,
roses and feathers
that tickled her face.
She clung to it bravely
but – doom and dismay –
the wind whistled through it
and blew it
away.

Hairy Maclary,
as quick as a flash,
was off on a desperate,
daredevil
dash.
Like lightning he scooted,
skedaddle-skeddoo,
while faster and faster,
the hat simply
FLEW.

He chased it through marigolds,
over a frond,
straight through the hedge
to the edge
of the pond.

THEN
with a swoop
and a flurry of black,
he caught it
and carried it …

ALL the way
back.

Hairy Maclary's Rumpus at the Vet

Down at the Vet's
there were all kinds of pets,
with troubles and woes
from their ears to their toes.
Sniffles and snuffles
and doses of flu,
itches and stitches
and tummy ache too.
So many animals,
watchful and wary,
and Hairy Maclary
from Donaldson's Dairy.

There were miserable dogs,
cantankerous cats,
a rabbit with pimples
and rickety rats.
Mice with the sneezes,
a goat in a rage,
and Cassie the cockatoo
locked in her cage.

Cassie had claws
and a troublesome beak.
She saw something twitch
so she gave it a
TWEAK.

She pulled it so hard
that she plucked out a hair
and Hairy Maclary
jumped high in the air.

A bowl full of mice
was bundled about.
Over it went
and the mice tumbled out.

Four fussy budgies
with Grandmother Goff
flew out of their cage
when the bottom dropped off.

Grizzly MacDuff
with a bottlebrush tail
leaped out of his basket
and over the rail.

The Poppadum kittens
from Parkinson Place
squeezed through an opening
and joined in the chase.

Barnacle Beasley
forgot he was sore.
He bumbled and clattered
all over the floor.

Then Custard the labrador,
Muffin McLay
and Noodle the poodle
decided to play.
They skidded and scampered,
they slid all around
and bottles and boxes
came tumbling down.

What a kerfuffle,
a scramble of paws,
a tangle of bodies,
a jumble of jaws.
With squawking and yowling
and mournful miaow,
they really were making
a TERRIBLE row.

Out came the Vet.
'I'll fix them,' she said.
But she tripped on a lead
and fell over instead.

Geezer the goat
crashed into a cage.
He butted the bars
in a thundering rage.

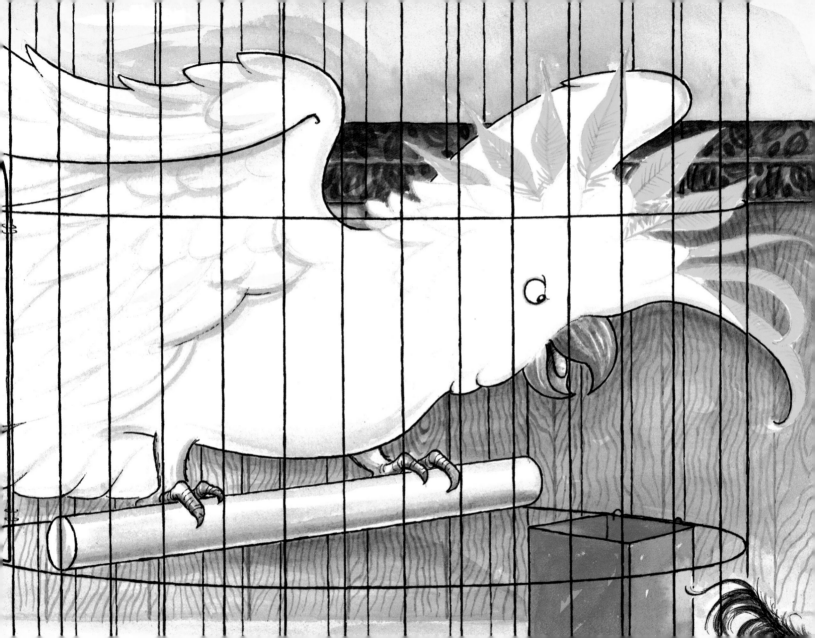

Cassie got mad.
She rattled her beak.
She saw something twitch
so she
gave
it
a ...

TWEAK.

Hairy Maclary, Shoo

Hairy Maclary
was having some fun,
messing about
with his friends
in the sun.
Frisky and skittish,
they romped
and they ran,
when . . .

up came a dusty
delivery van.
Off went the driver
with cartons of soup
SO
Hairy Maclary
decided to
snoop.

Back came the driver
and SLAM went the door.
Off went the van
with a rattle and roar;
way past the park
and the slippery slide,
uphill
and downhill –
with Hairy
inside.

Round every corner
they wobbled and bopped
till,
far from the Dairy,
they finally stopped.
One parcel more
for a furniture store
BUT
Hairy Maclary
shot out of the door.

Into a toyshop
he skidded and spun,
scattering blocks
as he slid on his tum.
Teddy bears tumbled
and fell on his head,
all in a jumble,
till somebody said . . .

'STOP this shemozzle,
this hullabaloo!
Scarper,
skedaddle,
BE OFF WITH YOU –
SHOO!'

Straight through the gate
of Magnolia School,
raced Hairy Maclary
round playground and pool.
Through every classroom
he wickedly sped
till,
outside his office,
the headmaster
said . . .

'STOP this shemozzle,
this hullabaloo!
Scarper,
skedaddle,
BE OFF WITH YOU –
SHOO!'

Over to Gulliver's
Garden Supplies,
rushed Hairy Maclary
with scaredy-cat eyes.
Tangled in creepers,
he panicked and fled
through palm trees
and poppies,
till everyone said . . .

'STOP this shemozzle,
this hullabaloo!
Scarper,
skedaddle,
BE OFF WITH YOU –
SHOO!'

Hairy Maclary
was tired of the fun.
His whiskers were draggled,
his collar undone.
He hid between flowerpots,
sad and alone,
waiting for someone
to show the way
home.
Wearily woeful
and gloomily glum,
he gave a deep sigh –
then . . .

along came Miss Plum.
'It's HAIRY MACLARY –
good gracious!'
she said,
scooping him up
with a pat on his head.
'My,
what a raggedy rascal you are,'
she laughed
as she trundled him
out to her car.

A wag of his tail
and a fidgety toe
meant Hairy Maclary
was ready
to go.

He watched as they drove
over Butterfly Bridge,
up the long hill
over Rollaway Ridge,
down past the park
with its zigzaggy bends,
back to the Dairy . . .

and back
to his friends.